The Lighthouse Keeper's New Friend

Ronda & David Armitage

SCHOLASTIC

First published in 2008 by Scholastic Children's Books
Euston House, 24 Eversholt Street
London NW1 1DB
a division of Scholastic Ltd
www.scholastic.co.uk
London ~ New York ~ Toronto ~ Sydney ~ Auckland
Mexico City ~ New Delhi ~ Hong Kong

Text copyright © 2008 Ronda Armitage
Illustrations copyright © 2008 David Armitage

ISBN 978 1407 10546 8

7 9 10 8

The moral rights of
Ronda Armitage and David Armitage have been asserted.

Papers used by Scholastic Children's Books are made from
wood grown in sustainable forests.

Mr and Mrs Grinling lived
with their cat, Hamish, in a
little white cottage perched high
on the cliffs. Mr Grinling was
a part-time lighthouse keeper.
He shared the work with his
assistant, Sam.

It was Monday and Monday was Mr Grinling's day off. Mrs Grinling was bustling about the kitchen and Mr Grinling was getting in the way. Well, Mrs Grinling thought he was getting in the way. Mr Grinling thought he was quietly eating his toast.

"Please eat faster, Mr G,"
said Mrs Grinling. "It's only
three weeks until Sam's wedding
and I haven't done any of
the cooking."

"Oh yummy," said Mr Grinling.
"I'll help."

"No, thank you," said Mrs Grinling. "You're a lovely man, Mr G, but a dreadful cook. You're much better at eating. Why don't you go and look for a mermaid instead?"

That's what's called a "private joke". Mr Grinling had always hoped that one day he might see a mermaid combing her golden hair.

There's nothing very unusual about that. Lots of people would like to see a mermaid. When Mr Grinling got in her way, Mrs Grinling often sent him to look for mermaids.

Meanwhile, something unusual was happening down in Wild Horses Bay. A small, golden shape was climbing out of the sea.

Sam saw it first.
He was cleaning
the lighthouse and
dreaming of Sally
de la Croissant.
In three weeks'
time they would
hold their wedding
at the lighthouse so
it needed to be spic
and span.
As he checked for ships
and boats through his telescope
he spied the small golden,
rather hairy thing on the rock.
"Funny colour for a seal,"
he thought.

Mr Grinling saw it, but not until later. He had decided to go surfing. As he walked down to Wild Horses Bay, he was thinking about the wedding too. He was to be the best man, which meant he had to wear a suit. He hated wearing suits.

He wished that Sam and Sally would just sail away in a beautiful pea green boat and forget about having a wedding.

Mrs Grinling didn't see the small hairy thing. She was making a list of the wedding food so she didn't have time to look outside.

It was while he was waiting for a big wave that Mr Grinling saw it. The sun glinted on the golden hair. Mr Grinling crossed his fingers.

Maybe, at last, he would see
a mermaid. He paddled towards
the rock but the closer he
got, the more disappointed
he became.

The creature was golden and
hairy but not like a mermaid.

"Next time," said Mr Grinling.
"Perhaps next time it just might
be a mermaid."

The small golden hairy thing lifted its head.

"Woof," it said quietly.

"That's definitely not a mermaid," sighed Mr Grinling. "Perhaps it's a merdog. You can't stay on this rock, little dog. It will be under water when the tide comes in."

He put the dog on the surfboard and paddled for the beach.

The little dog flopped onto the sand.

"Time for you to go home now," said Mr Grinling. "Home."

But the dog just gazed up at him with large mournful eyes.

"You must have a home," said Mr Grinling. "Most of us have homes somewhere.

"I can't take you to mine because Mrs G doesn't like dogs. She particularly doesn't like small, hairy and very smelly dogs. You do pong. Now please, go home."

Mr Grinling gave the little dog a pat and set off for his cottage.

Meanwhile, Sam was looking through his telescope again. He noticed that as Mr Grinling walked up the path, the small golden thing followed behind, just out of sight.

"Of course," he said to himself. "It's a dog. That spells T-R-O-U-B-L-E with Mrs G and Hamish."

It was lunch time in the little white cottage. Mr Grinling was eating fish pie and Mrs Grinling was still bustling about.

She stopped.

"I rescued him from the rock," explained Mr Grinling. "I did tell him to go home."

"Well, he can't have a home here," said Mrs Grinling. "Go away, dog."

But the little dog was so tired
he'd fallen asleep.

Mr Grinling gathered him
up and put him in Hamish's
old basket.

"Hamish won't like this either,"
said Mrs Grinling. "That dog
must go."

Mr Grinling sighed. He rather
liked the sad little dog.

Hamish did not like the little dog. He arched his orange back and spat, but the little dog took no notice. He wasn't frightened of cats.

"That dog cannot stay here,"
said Mrs Grinling over and over.
At least ten times that afternoon.

Mrs Grinling put up a large notice in the Lighthouse Bay shop, but nobody came to collect the dog.

It was Thursday and breakfast time again. There was a lot of barking and squawking in the garden. Mrs Grinling smiled.

"The only thing that dog is good for is chasing seagulls. I don't like him, Mr G, but it looks as though he's here to stay. There are three conditions…"

bath so he

ong.

3

You encourage him to chase the seagulls.

Dog wagged his tail. Mr Grinling would have wagged his too if he'd had one. Instead he hugged the dog and Mrs Grinling, and announced that from now on dog was called Merdog.

"I found him on a rock," he explained to anyone who asked. "He might have come from the sea."

Mr Grinling and Merdog became good friends.

Mrs Grinling and Merdog
did not become good friends.
Merdog did not understand the
bathing bit. He loved being dirty.

Merdog did not understand the
kitchen rule either. He thought
that if humans came into
kitchens and ate off tables
then dogs should too.

OUT! OUT!

"That dog," muttered Mrs
Grinling darkly as she chased
him out.

Merdog did understand about chasing seagulls. He chased them whenever they flew into the garden.

He also tried chasing Hamish,
but a sharp tap on the nose soon
fixed that.

Merdog followed Mr Grinling
everywhere. He thought
Mr Grinling was "the bee's knees".
It was Monday again and
Sam was looking through
his telescope. He observed
Mr Grinling on his surfboard
with a small golden hairy thing.

"Well I never," said Sam to
himself. "That dog is surfing."
And because he liked talking
to himself he added,
    "Perhaps it really is a merdog.
Perhaps it did just come
from the sea."

And now there's another bit to
this story…

Far away in a town, Louis,
aged eight, cried himself to
sleep again. He had lost a
very good friend.

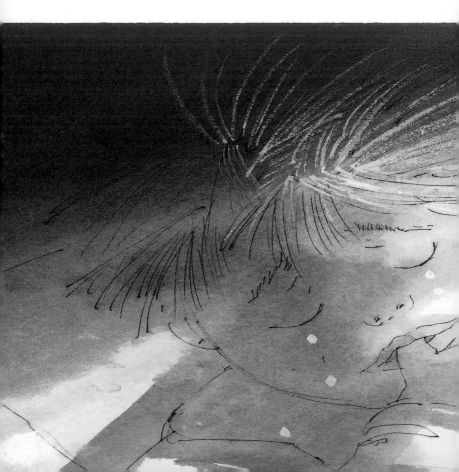

His mother and father had looked everywhere for this friend, but he had vanished. Louis had cried himself to sleep for nine nights.

It was Monday again and only five days to the wedding. Mrs Grinling was extremely busy. The freezer was full of food but there was still more cooking to do. . .

1 Make lots of sausage rolls...

2 get four fish pies...

Again it was Mr Grinling's day off and again he was in Mrs Grinling's way.

"Please Mr G," she said. "Go and find a mermaid for Merdog. I am so busy I can't think straight."

She was searching in the fridge.

"Oh no," she wailed. "I've run out of butter and Lighthouse Bay shop is closed today."

"Then Merdog and I will cycle to Wild Horses Bay Stores," said Mr Grinling.

But there was a surprise
waiting when Mr Grinling and
Merdog puffed into the village.
Well, Mr Grinling was puffing;
Merdog was snoozing in the
bike basket.

There in the shop window was
a large poster.

Bob, our
golden dog, is
missing. Maybe
he has run away
to sea. Our son Louis
is heartbroken. If you
find him please ring
07757575881.

What a nasty surprise
for Mr Grinling. Merdog
couldn't stay with him. He
belonged to Louis, who
was very upset.

"We'll run away together,"
whispered Mr Grinling to
Merdog. "We'll hide in
the woods."

He cycled quickly down
the street. But he didn't go
far. He didn't even reach
the first tree. He couldn't
keep Merdog when Louis
was so unhappy.

He cycled back up the
street again.

The shopkeeper was outside
the door.

"You've found Bob then," he
said. "He's always running away.
He doesn't like living in the town,
you see, so whenever the Loppits
return home after their holiday,
Bob vanishes."

Bob barked when he heard
his name.

Bob, our
golden dog, is
missing. Maybe
he has run away
to sea. Our son Louis
is heartbroken. If you
find him please ring
07757575881.

Bob

"I'll really miss him," sighed Mr
Grinling. "We're good friends,
Merdog – I mean Bob – and I.
I rescued him from a rock, you
know, and I've taught him to surf.
He's a real sea dog."

So he wrote down Louis'
telephone number and he and
Merdog-called-Bob cycled
for home.

Every now and then he would
pat Merdog in the basket
behind. This was not a good
idea when on a bicycle.

It was also not a good idea for
a dog to leap up and down in a
bike basket. As they cycled down
the hill, the bike wobbled and
tipped and Mr Grinling went
sprawling across the road.

"I can't move my leg," he groaned. Merdog sat beside him. He licked Mr Grinling's face as if to say, "Don't worry, I'll look after you."

Three seagulls hovered above the accident.

At first Merdog tried to ignore the seagulls. He wanted to look after Mr Grinling.

But he was a dog, after all.

Bit by bit the seagulls tempted him to follow them. He chased them all the way to the little white cottage where Mrs Grinling was waiting for the butter.

"Mr G!" cried Mrs Grinling. "You foolish man. What have you done?"

Now things happened very
quickly. The helicopter rescued
Mr Grinling and took him into
hospital with Mrs Grinling (and
Merdog of course).

Somehow the newspaper heard about the rescue so Merdog had his photo in the paper. Even Mrs Grinling agreed that Merdog was a hero.

The next day, Mr Grinling came home again with his leg in plaster.

Then it was Saturday, and that meant the wedding. The sun was shining as it always does in the best stories.

Mr Grinling, the hop-along best man, was dressed in his lighthouse clothes. His broken leg wouldn't fit into the suit.

On a boat just out from the lighthouse an eight-year-old boy called Louis looked through a telescope.

Yes, Mr Grinling had remembered to ring him.

"I can see my dog," shouted Louis. "Bob, Bob!"

"Merdog, Merdog!" cried Mr Grinling.

What confusion. There's a bride and groom who have just been married, lots of guests who are hungry, and a small, hairy dog swimming backwards and forwards between the two people he loves.

At last it was all sorted out. Sally invited Louis and his mum and dad to the wedding so Bob or Merdog could be with his best friends.

Mr Grinling and Louis decided they could share the little dog. This was very hard for Louis, but he knew that Bob hated living in the town. He was a sea dog through and through.

Bob stays with Louis in his holiday house at the weekends, and Mr Grinling looks after Merdog during the week. Two dog names, but the little golden dog is very happy.

Mrs Grinling has become quite
fond of Merdog, but Hamish
is still cross.

"That dog!" he spits.